58.95

8/20/13

Greek Mythology's Adventures of

ACKNOWLEDGEMENTS

Special thanks to Raymond Minnaar for the use of his artwork for promotional purposes.

Edited by Ryan Jacobson
Cover art by Elizabeth Hurley

10 9 8 7 6 5 4 3 2 1

Library of Congress Control Number: 2012909957

Copyright 2013 by Blake Hoena
Published by Lake 7 Creative, LLC
Minneapolis, MN 55412
www.lake7creative.com

All rights reserved
Printed in the U.S.A.

ISBN: 978-0-9821187-9-5

DEAR READER,

I've always been a fan of superheroes: Spider-man, Batman, and countless others. I've read tons of comic books, seen all of the superhero movies, and even written a few books about some popular superheroes.

Most people don't realize that the world's first superheroes came from Greek myths. Hercules and Theseus were models for our current superheroes. They were stronger and faster than normal people. In their stories, power from the Greek gods made them "super." Today, you can see characters from myth, like Hercules and Ares, popping up in comics.

Perseus is the character that started it all. He was the first well-known Greek hero, and he's what the ancient Greeks thought a hero should be. Perseus is good and honest, and he tries to help others.

His story is one of my favorites, so I am thrilled to adapt it into a Choose Your Path book. Now you can experience the dangers that Perseus faced, and you can battle your own monsters. I hope you enjoy my retelling of his story.

— Blake Hoena

HOW TO USE THIS BOOK

As you read *Greek Mythology's Adventures of Perseus*, you will sometimes be asked to jump to a distant page. Please follow these instructions. Sometimes you will be asked to choose between two or more options. Decide which you feel is best, and go to the corresponding page. (But be careful; some options will lead to disaster.) Finally, if a page offers no instructions or choices, just turn to the next page.

Enjoy the story, and good luck!

TABLE OF CONTENTS

GREEK NAMES AND PLACES

In this story, you will meet ancient Greek people and visit some strange places. The words may seem difficult to say, but this guide will teach you how to pronounce them correctly.

Acrisius (*uh-kriss-EE-us*)—grandfather of Perseus and king of Argos

Andromeda (*an-DROM-eh-duh*)—daughter of Queen Cassiopeia and King Cepheus

Argos (*AR-goes*)—ancient Greek city

Atlas (*AT-less*)—Titan who holds up the heavens

Athena (*uh-THEE-nuh*)—goddess of war and protector of heroes

Cassiopeia (*kass-ee-oh-PEE-uh*)—queen of a kingdom in Africa

Cepheus (*see-FEE-us*)—king of a kingdom in Africa

Danae (*DAN-ay-ee*)—mother of Perseus

Dictys (*DIK-tiss*)—fisherman and friend of Perseus

Hermes (*HER-meez*)—messenger of the gods

Medusa (*meh-DOO-suh*)—monster whose gaze turns people into stone

Perseus (*PUR-see-us*)—hero and star of this story

Polydectes (*pol-ee-DEK-teez*)—ruler of Seriphus

Poseidon (*poe-SYE-dun*)—god of the sea

Seriphus (*sur-EH-fuss*)—ancient island near Greece

Zeus (*ZOOSS*)—ruler of the gods and father of Perseus

PROLOGUE:
LIBRARY FINDS

You biked to the public library straight from school. They just got the new *Muscle Man* graphic novel. He's your favorite superhero.

You hunker down in a cushy chair. You're about to crack open the book when you notice a high schooler digging through the graphic novel shelves. You watch him closely. It's always cool to know what the older kids are reading.

He loads up with half a dozen books in one arm. With his free hand, he reaches into his back pocket and pulls out his wallet. You watch him fumble for a few seconds while trying to balance all of his books. Then he finds his library card.

He tries to stuff his wallet back into his pocket, but he misses. His wallet lands silently on the carpeted floor. You watch curiously as the teenager walks away. He doesn't realize what happened.

You walk over and pick up the wallet. You glance around. No one sees you, so you carefully thumb it open. There are several twenty-dollar bills in it. With that, you could buy the whole *Muscle Man* series.

Hissss!

You spin around, thinking you're about to be bitten by venomous vipers. Nothing.

Hissss!

There it is again, coming from another section of books. You mindlessly tuck the wallet into your front pocket, and you sneak toward the sound.

The noise grows louder, and it's not just a hissing sound anymore. You hear the crashing of waves and a woman pleading, "No, please, no!"

You rush around a bookshelf, expecting to find someone in danger. Instead, all that stands before you is a wall of old books. This is a part of the library you never visit. It's the classics section. Battered books line the shelves: *The Call of the Wild*, *Treasure Island*, *20,000 Leagues Under the Sea* and many more.

Hissss!

You jump back, thinking you're about to be bitten by a snake. That's when you notice a book lying at your feet: *Metamorphoses* by Ovid. It's older and more tattered than the rest of the books. Suddenly, you realize that the strange sounds are coming from its pages.

The only way to find out what's going on is to pick up the book. But you're afraid to guess what will happen if you do. You sense that it could be dangerous. Yet it could also lead to the adventure of a lifetime.

The noises begin to fade. Your instincts tell you that it's now or never. You must decide, and you must decide fast. Will you pick up the book, or will you leave it be? What will you choose to do?

To pick up the book, go to page 27.

To leave the book, go to page 21.

You look at your mother. There's sadness in her eyes. You know she wants to live in a palace again. But she doesn't love Polydectes, so you must offer something else.

"I have nothing of value to give you," you say. "But if there is something you want, name it and I will get it for you."

The king's expression is hard to read. You don't know if you have impressed him or made some deadly mistake. The crowd quiets as they wait for Polydectes to respond. A wicked smile crosses the king's lips, and you fear that you may have gone too far with your boast.

"Bring me Medusa's head!" Polydectes exclaims.

The crowd is stunned, and you feel everyone slowly shrink away from you. Everyone except your mother. A look of horror strikes her.

"If that is what you desire," you say, even though fear causes your knees to tremble.

"It is," the king replies.

You begin to walk away, but you are jerked back around as your mother yanks your arm.

"Perseus, you can't do this," she cries. "No one has ever come back from Medusa's lair!"

You know that you've been tricked by Polydectes, but you made a promise. "Mother, I have to do this," you tell her. "If I don't, Polydectes will never leave us alone. We won't be safe on Seriphus. The king might even harm Dictys if we don't do as he commands."

You wish you could do more to calm your mother. But if you stay too long, fear may get the best of you. That would give Polydectes another chance to embarrass you in front of his wealthy guests.

"Mother," you say, "if I am the son of Zeus, as you once told me, then I stand a chance of returning."

"And until you do," Polydectes interrupts, "your mother will stay with me."

Guards surround you. They are armed with long spears, and you know now that you have no choice. You must leave your mother with Polydectes and hope that she isn't harmed while you're on your quest.

"I will give you a month," the king adds. "If you don't return with Medusa's head, I will marry your mother."

You exchange an angry glare with the king, and then you quickly walk away. Your mother's sobs break the silence.

Your strides are long and purposeful. You cannot wait to get away from the king and his laughing, rich guests.

Once beyond the palace walls, you hear someone call your name. "Perseus, wait," a woman yells. "I have something to tell you."

You glance back. The woman calling after you looks almost queen-like. She wears white robes with a golden clasp shaped like an owl.

She looks like one of Polydectes's guests. Did he send her to trick and embarrass you further? Or might she be someone who wishes to help? You could use any help you can get. But the person you really want to talk to is Dictys. Maybe he'll know what to do next. Should you take a moment to speak with this woman, or should you hurry away? What will you choose to do?

To talk with the woman, go to page 32.

To find Dictys right away, go to page 74.

Polydectes has a palace full of guards. There is no way to rescue your mother. Your only hope is to succeed in your quest. And quickly.

"First you must get a good night's rest," Dictys says. "Tomorrow, we'll find you a ship that will take you across the sea."

That night, you dream of walking through a barren land. There are no trees, no shrubs, no grass. The ground is baked and cracked. You don't lack for food or drink, but you don't seem to get any nearer to the end of your quest. You continue to walk. And walk. And walk. The land is never ending, and it never changes.

"You didn't choose wisely," a voice says from above. You look up to see an owl soaring overhead. Athena?

The next morning, Dictys offers to help you find a boat. But your dream has made you realize something. Even if you can sail to the land of Atlas, you could never get to Medusa's lair on foot. You need to go back to the Nymphs of the North and re-choose your items.

You pack as much as you can carry, and you walk north. Days pass, and you eventually find the clearing, the dark cave, and the Nymphs of the North.

"Perseus, we've been expecting you," one of them sings. "You chose poorly."

"You will need one item from each of us to complete your quest," another nymph sings.

"Choose wisely," they sing together.

Go to the next page.

Write on a piece of paper the items you choose, so you will remember them during your quest.

The first nymph holds out her gift. "The cup of the gods," she says, "and the winged sandals. You can only keep one. Which will you choose?"

The second nymph holds out her gift. "The helmet or the bow and arrows," she says. "You can only keep one. Which will you choose?"

The third nymph holds out her gift. "The pouch and the ring," she says. "You can only keep one. Which will you choose?"

When you have decided, go to the next page.

"Thank you for your gifts," you tell the nymphs. "It is a long way to travel, and I should get started."

If you have the winged sandals, go to page 60.

If you do not have winged sandals, go to page 22.

Athena has chosen to help you because you are a hero. You will act like one and do what is right. But you still need to be cautious.

"Here," you shout.

The three witches tilt their heads to the sound of your voice. You toss the eye toward the back of the cave. It lands with a squeak, and all three witches spin toward the sound of it.

You turn from them and flee out of the cave. You leap into the air. The flutter of your winged sandals lifts you skyward.

Behind, deep within the cave, you hear the three witches screeching.

"Here it is!"

"That's a rock!"

"Keep looking. Keep looking!"

4
MEDUSA'S
LAIR

You know where Medusa lives. With that knowledge, you believe that you can complete your quest. You are hopeful that you will get back to Seriphus in time to keep Polydectes from marrying your mother.

As you fly south, the sky gets darker. Rolling black clouds block out the sun. Soon, you no longer see a hint of blue in the sky.

Beneath you, the land changes from green to gray. The rich African grasslands give way to barren land. No trees. No grass. No animals. Everything below you is gray and lifeless. On either side of you, the ground falls away into nothing. Eventually, the land becomes a thin peninsula stretching across a dark void.

Ahead, you see a rocky hill rise above the lifeless landscape. Beyond that, the world just seems to end. There is only blackness.

The Gray Witches said you would find Medusa at the end of the earth: where the sun never shines and the moon is never seen. Here, there is no sun and no moon. This must be Medusa's lair.

At the foot of the hill is a path. It leads to a plateau on top of the hill. You could fly to the top. That would save you some time, and you might be able to surprise Medusa. Or you could land at the bottom of the hill. It would take longer, but that would allow you more time to prepare. What will you choose to do?

To land on top of the hill, go to page 64.

To land at the foot of the hill, go to page 90.

Thoughts of adventure and life-or-death choices? Not for you. Besides, you're probably just being silly. You decide to leave the book alone. You have a more important decision to worry about: what to do with the wallet. Should you keep it, or should you give it back?

In the end, you figure that it's too late to return it. The older boy probably realized that he dropped it. He might be looking for it now. You don't want to imagine what he'd do if he saw you with it.

You go back to your seat. As you pick up the graphic novel, you wonder what your favorite superhero, Muscle Man, would have done. A painful guilt gnaws at your stomach. It twists and tightens and makes you feel sick. Deep down inside, you know the right thing to do. Unfortunately, you don't have the courage to do it.

Go to page 67.

You did not select the winged sandals, so you have no option but to start walking. You thank Hermes for his help and begin trudging back through the forest.

Eventually you come to the twisting animal trails that you traveled on days before. Then the roads. You feel confident that you are on the right path.

After a few days, you reach your home with Dictys. You'll need a boat to get off the island, and Dictys knows all of the sailors and fishermen on Seriphus. One of them might be willing to help you sail south.

Dictys is confused and happy to see you. "Did you slay Medusa already?" he asks.

"No, I've only seen the Nymphs of the North," you reply. Then you show him the items that you selected, along with Hermes's sword and Athena's shield.

Before you can ask Dictys about finding a ship, he tells you, "I have heard a rumor. I don't know if it's true, but it's been said that Polydectes is planning to wed your mother while you are off on your quest. He has set a wedding date for next week."

The news makes you angry. Can you continue on your quest without knowing that your mother is safe? She means everything to you. Your instincts tell you that you should go and help her. However, you could also help her by quickly completing your quest. Is this even possible? Do you have enough time? What will you choose to do?

To return to your mother, go to page 42.

To continue on your quest, go to page 14.

You decide to sneak up on the witches. They are so focused on their dinner that you doubt they will notice you. Quietly, you walk toward them.

"Give me the eye," the third witch hisses. "I want to make sure you aren't overcooking the stew."

"It's fine," the first witch says.

"Give me the tooth, so I can taste it," demands the second witch.

With a *smuck*, the first witch pulls the tooth from her gums and hands it to the second witch.

With a *slurp*, the tooth slides into her gums. She scoops up a spoonful of stew. On the spoon is a leg bone that looks like it could be a person's. She grabs it and starts chomping. *Crunch! Crunch! Crunch!*

Looking around the cavern, you see only old clothes and bones. The witches don't seem to have any treasures. However, there are two things that they value greatly: the tooth and the eye. Maybe if you took one of them, they would tell you where Medusa lives.

But which do they value more, the eye or the tooth? If you take the eye, they won't be able to see the food that they're preparing. They won't be able to see you either. Without the tooth, they won't be able to eat their stew. The tooth also seems to be their only weapon. What will you choose to do?

To take the eye, go to page 80.

To take the tooth, go to page 76.

You are thankful that you chose the winged sandals. They are what Hermes uses to fly around as messenger of the gods. Without them, it could take a long time to reach the land where Atlas holds up the heavens. With them, it will be a matter of minutes.

Just think about where you want to go, says a voice in your head. It sounds strangely like Athena. *The sandals will take you there.*

You think of Atlas. The wings on your sandals begin to flutter. First your left leg and then your right lifts off the ground. You wobble as you struggle to keep your balance, but slowly you rise upward.

You're not sure if this is safer than walking, but it's too late. You are a hundred feet off the ground. The only way to go is onward.

You lean in the direction you want to fly. You hear the wings begin to whir, and you are pushed forward with the wind whipping your hair. The ground below you becomes a blur.

Go to page 61.

You decide to pick up the book. What could be more exciting than adventure and life-or-death choices?

The book is thicker and heavier than you expected. It sends a tingling shock through your fingers.

Then the strange noises surround you: the hissing, the crashing waves, the woman crying. They are deafening. They drown out all other sounds.

The book flips open. You see the bolded words, *The Story of Perseus*. The page begins to glow, and you can't look away. As you stare at the words, you grow dizzy. Your head begins to swirl. Your legs tremble. You fall forward, into the book, and everything goes black.

1

THE ISLAND OF SERIPHUS

You cry out in alarm.

"Perseus, what's wrong?" a woman calls to you. She is your mother, Danae.

Her soft, warm arms reach out for you. They pull you near, and you curl into her embrace. As she hugs you, you feel heavy sobs shake your mother's body.

The two of you are in a large box. It's tall enough for you to sit in but not large enough for you to stand.

A sliver of light shines through a crack in the box's lid. You're able to see the faint outline of your mother. She looks as if she's been crying for days.

Her body tenses. She takes a deep breath. She squeezes you tightly and says, "I must tell you why we are here."

Your eyes widen with surprise. Your mother has been guarding this secret from you. Now you eagerly await the truth.

"We live in Greece. It is a world of gods, magic, and monsters," she says. "As you know, your grandfather is King Acrisius, ruler of the city of Argos. He had us put into this box."

You gasp in surprise.

Your mother continues. "King Acrisius once had his future told to him. It was said that his grandson would be the cause of his death. So he locked me in a tower and never let me see anyone. He hoped I would never fall in love—and never have children. But Zeus, the ruler of the gods, can do anything. He flew into the tower and visited me. We had a child together: you."

"My father is a Greek god?" you exclaim.

Your mother nods. "For years I hid you from your grandfather, and we lived happily in the tower. But one day, not long ago, the king heard you laughing. When he saw you in the tower, he was afraid."

"That I would cause his death," you whisper.

"Yes," your mother answers. "He had us put into this

chest and set adrift at sea. The king hopes to never see either of us again." After that, she says no more.

You are trapped. The chest rocks as it is tossed by the waves. You press further into your mother's arms to soothe your fears and to comfort her.

The wind whispers above the crashing waves. You hear your name in those whispers. *Perseus, don't be afraid.* The voice is comforting. You are lulled to sleep by its fatherly tone.

You wake as a shudder vibrates through the chest.

What happened? Did you strike a rock? Will you sink? The worries race through your mind.

The chest isn't leaking water, and the rocking has stopped. You turn to your mother. She has one finger raised to her lips.

"Shhhh," she whispers.

Then you hear a man speak.

"What kind of treasure is this?" he says.

The man grunts, and you feel the chest being dragged along the ground of some sandy beach.

Loud clangs ring out. The man must be hammering

at the lock that holds the chest closed.

You look to your mother. Her eyes are wide with fear. She has protected you all your life. Now it's your turn to protect her. You kneel in front of her and face the lid of the chest.

Klunk! The lock has been broken. Slowly, the lid begins to open.

You're in a strange land. You have no way of knowing if the man opening the chest is friendly or not. Should you attack? Or should you wait to see if he's kind? Attacking a stranger is a dangerous move. You don't know what you're up against. But if you wait, and if he is a villain, you might not stand a chance. What will you choose to do?

To attack the man, go to page 40.

To see if the man is friendly, go to page 54.

Without help, no matter from whom, you will never be able to succeed on your quest. You turn to see what the woman wants.

As she approaches, you notice odd things about her. There's a slight glow around her, and her feet do not touch the ground. She glides across the grass when she walks, and she wears an owl clasp as her symbol.

"Perseus, do you know who I am?" she asks.

"You are Athena," you quietly reply.

She nods. "I am here to help you."

You remember what Dictys told you about Athena. She's not just a goddess of war. She is also the protector of heroes.

"I will accept any offer of help you give," you say.

"Go and find the Nymphs of the North. They have items that will help you on your journey." After she says these words, she disappears.

You hurry home and quickly tell Dictys about what happened at the feast. His emotions are mixed. He's fearful of your impossible quest, but he sounds hopeful when you tell him that Athena offered to help.

"I've heard of the Nymphs of the North," he says. "You simply need to travel north. Eventually you will find them."

"That doesn't sound too hard," you say.

"Maybe not," Dictys says. "But you'll only find them if they wish to be found."

"Oh." Worry taints your reply.

"If Athena is helping you . . ." his voice trails off. Dictys doesn't want to say anything that might make you afraid. After all, you have a long and difficult quest ahead of you.

The next day, you pack as much as you can carry, and you walk north. At first, there are well-worn paths to follow. Those paths narrow into twisting animal trails. Then the trails disappear completely. You find yourself winding your way through a thick forest.

Go to the next page.

Days pass. Your supplies run out. Thirst burns your throat. Hungers stabs your belly. You worry that you could die before your quest even begins.

You hear the sound of water and are drawn to it. You enter a clearing and come face to face with a rocky wall. At its base is a small pool of water. Beyond the pool, a dark cave cuts into the rock. And near the cave, three women await you: the Nymphs of the North.

"Perseus, we've been expecting you," one of them sings.

They stand as one and walk toward you. They are graceful beyond any human you've ever seen. They hold an object in each of their hands.

"We have gifts for you," another sings.

"You will need one item from each of us to complete your quest," the last one sings.

"Choose wisely," they sing together.

Go to the next page.

Write on a piece of paper the items you choose, so you will remember them during your quest.

The first nymph holds out a gold cup and a pair of winged sandals.

"This is the cup of the gods," she says. "You have a long journey ahead, and you will need nourishment if you are to survive. The cup will always be full when you need a drink or a bite to eat.

"The winged sandals will allow you to fly anywhere in the world, and quickly. Medusa's lair is far, far away. Your journey could take a long time. And unless you know someone with a boat, you must find another way to travel."

You can only take one. Which will you choose?

When you have decided, go to the next page.

The second nymph holds out a helmet and a set of bow and arrows.

"This helmet can only be worn once, and it will make you invisible. In your darkest hour, you will be able to escape unseen from your enemies.

"These arrows never miss when shot from this bow. You'll face many dangers on your quest. This weapon provides great protection."

You can only take one. Which will you choose?

When you have decided, go to the next page.

The third nymph holds up a simple leather pouch and a plain, bronze ring.

"The pouch is magic," she says. "In it, you can safely carry anything. It does not matter how big, how small or what the item is made of. It will fit in the pouch, and it will be protected.

"The ring will save you from poison. You need not worry about anyone trying to taint your food or drink, and you will be protected from animal venom—such as the bite of Medusa's snake-hair."

You can only take one. Which will you choose?

When you have decided, go to the next page.

"Thank you for your gifts," you tell the nymphs. "How do I find Medusa?"

"We don't know," they sing.

"But I can help," a male voice says.

You spin around and see a traveler. He wears a hat adorned with wings. He has a bronze shield slung across his back and a sword belted around his waist.

"I am the messenger of the gods, Hermes," he says. "Athena sent me to help you on your quest." He grabs his sword and hands it to you. "This blade is strong enough to cut through Medusa's scaly hide."

You take the sword from Hermes and strap it around your waist.

Next, Hermes hands you the shield. "And this is Athena's shield. She hopes it will help you in battle."

You take the shield and sling it across your back. With the gifts from the nymphs and these weapons, you feel confident. But there is one thing you still lack: knowledge. "How do I find Medusa?" you ask.

"Travel south, across the sea, to the land where Atlas holds up the heavens. There, you will find the Gray Witches. They are sisters of Medusa, and they can tell you where she lives."

"It is a long way to reach them," Hermes says. "You should get started on your journey."

If you have the winged sandals, go to page 60.

If you do not have winged sandals, go to page 22.

It's too dangerous to wait and find out if the man is friendly. You clench your fists and prepare to fight.

You've been shut inside the dark chest for days. When the lid pops open, the outside light is blinding. All you can see is a dark shadow standing before you. You spring at it. And miss.

You land face down on a wet, sandy beach. Strong hands grip you and lift you up. You kick and scream.

The man sets you down gently on your feet. "Are you okay?" he asks with a laugh. He brushes the sand off your face.

You blink against the sunlight. Slowly your eyes adjust to the brightness. The man before you is tall and strong. His beard is scruffy. His clothes are ragged. His hands are rough and dirty. You can tell by the faint smell of fish that he is a fisherman.

"What a fine young lad," the man says with a smile. "Protecting your mother."

His face is kind, and you feel the worry leak from your body. Now you are simply tired. Very, very tired.

The man turns to your mother, who is still crouched in the chest.

"My name is Dictys," he says as he extends a hand to her. "Welcome to the island of Seriphus."

Dictys helps your mother from the chest and asks her what happened. How did she and her son end up locked in a chest and adrift at sea? Your mother tells the story of King Acrisius, and she introduces you.

"That is a sad tale," he whispers. "I will find you some clean clothes and food to eat back at my hut."

Go to page 56.

You don't trust Polydectes. You cannot leave your mother in his care. You must rescue her.

You storm off to the king's palace. There, you are greeted by guards—too many to fight. It's almost as if Polydectes was expecting you.

He walks to the palace grounds to greet you. Your mother is at his side. Her sad eyes are downcast, and she won't even meet your gaze.

"Where is Medusa's head?" Polydectes asks.

"I haven't completed my quest yet," you reply.

"Then you have failed," Polydectes says.

Anger boils within you. You reach for your sword, but the guards are quicker. They point several spears at your chest. One thrust would end your life.

"Polydectes, no!" your mother cries. "You promised not to harm him if I marry you."

"So I have," Polydectes says. "Guards, take his sword. Bring him to the stables. He'll be my new stable boy. He can spend the rest of his life cleaning up after my horses." He laughs a cruel laugh.

Quickly, the guards grab the items that the nymphs gave you, as well as Hermes's gifts. Without them, you have no hope of completing your quest or preventing Polydectes from marrying your mother.

She is led away, disappearing into the palace with Polydectes. You are brought to the stables.

The work is hard. And you aren't even invited to your mother's wedding. You and the other stable hands can only listen to the cheers of celebration from outside the palace.

You almost never see your mother. When you do, her face is sad. There are always guards near her. They block your path any time you step in her direction.

You made a terrible mistake. Because of it, you must spend the rest of your lonely life working for Polydectes and missing your mother.

Go to page 67.

You turn to your mother and ask if she is willing to marry Polydectes, if she will be your gift for the king. You tell her that she'll live in a castle again. And even though you're not sure you want her to, you hope she says yes, just so your embarrassment ends.

There is a determined look in your mother's eyes. She nods. "If that's what you wish, Perseus."

Shouting above the crowd, you announce, "You're right. I did bring my mother as your gift. She's agreed to marry you, to be your queen." Quickly, the mood of the crowd changes. Instead of laughing at you, people congratulate you.

You are led inside, and it's a wonderful party. There are jugglers and storytellers. There's as much food as you can eat—food other than fish. For the first time in a long time, your belly feels full.

You notice your mother standing next to Polydectes. She doesn't look happy. But when your eyes meet, she fakes a smile.

You wonder if you made the right choice. You don't think you did. But before you can tell her she doesn't have to marry Polydectes, the king approaches you.

"As a reward for your kind gift," he says, "I have found work for you as a stable boy. You will clean up after my horses. You'll have a bed to sleep in and food to eat." He laughs and then walks away.

The work is hard. And you aren't even invited to your mother's wedding. You and the other stable hands can only listen to the cheers of celebration from outside the palace.

You almost never see your mother. When you do, her face is sad. There are always guards near her. They block your path any time you step in her direction.

You made a terrible mistake. Because of it, you must spend the rest of your lonely life working for Polydectes and missing your mother.

Go to page 67.

You have no choice. You need to complete your quest quickly. You agree to Atlas's demand.

He lifts the heavens off his shoulders and sets it on yours. You brace yourself for the crushing weight that bears down on you. It's heavier than you could have imagined. Your shoulders and back begin to ache at once. Your legs shake from the strain. Sweat covers your entire body.

"I don't know how long I can hold it," you gasp.

"You must or you will be crushed," the Titan says. He rubs his shoulders and stretches his back.

"Please," you gasp. "Where are the Gray Witches?"

Atlas scans the horizon. Then he points off into the distance. You follow his line of sight and see a small black speck, a cave, at the base of one of the mountains.

You feel relieved, knowing that you can continue on with your quest. "Are you ready to take the heavens back?" you ask.

Atlas smiles wickedly. "No, son of Zeus. I can see your father in you, and this is my revenge upon him. You have willingly taken my burden. It's now yours to bear." He turns and marches down the side of the mountain.

You call after him, but with the weight of the heavens upon you, you find it hard to yell.

Atlas's giant strides quickly take him out of earshot. You are left on your own, at the top of the highest peak of this mountain range.

No matter how you adjust your feet, your arms, your shoulders, the crushing weight doesn't feel any more comfortable. A sense of hopelessness sinks in.

Seconds pass. Minutes. Hours. And ever so slowly, days, weeks, months, and years. Sand and rock pile up at your feet. You are eventually buried, but you live on.

The spot where you stand becomes known as Mount Perseus. You could take pride in that, if only you knew your mother's fate.

Go to page 67.

You don't have time to be sneaky. Every moment you waste is another moment that your mom is with Polydectes. You worry that she is not safe with him.

Besides, you have nothing to fear from these three witches. They are old ladies with only one eye and one tooth between them.

If you have the bow and arrows, go to page 84.

If you do not, go to page 68.

You decide to stay with Dictys. He doesn't have much wealth or comfort to offer, but you trust him. You also feel indebted to Dictys. The only way to pay him back is to stay and help him.

"We will stay," you tell Polydectes.

His face drops in anger. He answers, "If you change your mind, you are welcome at my palace." The king says this not to you, but to your mother.

As he walks away, he turns toward you and scowls. You worry that you have just made an enemy—a very powerful enemy with an army at his command. You'll need to be careful around the king of Seriphus.

Dictys comes and hugs you. "You've become like a son to me," he says. "I'm glad you are staying."

You feel that you have made the right choice. But as you turn to your mother, she sighs and says, "It would be nice to live in a castle again."

2
AN IMPOSSIBLE QUEST

One day, you hear that Polydectes is holding a grand feast. A messenger delivers invitations to both you and your mother.

"But he didn't invite you," you say to Dictys.

"That's fine by me," Dictys says. "My brother and I don't get along very well."

You crumple up your invitation and toss it on the ground. "Then I won't go either," you say.

Dictys picks up the invitation. He carefully smooths it out and hands it back to you.

"The king isn't asking you to come. He's commanding it," Dictys warns. "He doesn't like you. It's best not to anger him further. You and your mother will go."

You trust Dictys and will do as he says, whether you like it or not.

"You must bring a gift," Dictys says. "It's a tradition to bring the host of a party some treasure."

"But I have nothing of value," you say.

Dictys doesn't offer any ideas. He just lowers his head and walks away.

When the day of the feast arrives, you are nervous. You haven't found anything to give Polydectes. But you go anyway, not wanting to anger the king.

At the entrance to his palace, you see Polydectes. He greets his guests as they hand him gifts. Golden goblets, beautiful horses, fine robes, and many other treasures surround the king.

"Perseus, you come with nothing," Polydectes says. "Or have you brought your mother to be my queen?"

As the king jokes, a crowd gathers around you. The people are well-dressed and have already given the king his gifts. They laugh at you, and you feel ashamed.

Maybe there is something that the king desires. Something he doesn't have. You could offer to get it for him. He'd be impressed by your courage. He also doesn't have a wife. Maybe your mother should marry him. She's not happy living with Dictys, and she likes the idea of living in a palace. You must offer something. What will you choose to do?

To get something for the king, go to page 11.

To ask your mother to marry him, go to page 44.

The witches are far too dangerous. You nearly fell into their grasp once. What if one of them could see you? Would she curse you with some spell, or worse?

"Sorry," you say as you turn from the witches. "But I've decided to keep your eye."

You leap into the air. Your winged sandals lift you upward—and just in time. Below, three shadows dart forward. They stop at the exact spot where you spoke your last words.

The witches blindly thrash and grope, smashing rocks with their fists. You hate to imagine what would have happened if they had caught you.

"Too late," you yell. "I'm off to slay Medusa."

"We curse you, Perseus," one of the witches hisses.

"We curse you for breaking your promise," another of them screeches.

"We curse you for keeping our precious eye," the third witch screams.

Then they all yell together, "May our sister turn you into stone!"

Go to page 19.

You've been shut inside the dark chest for days. You're weak and hungry. You don't have the strength to fight, so you kneel in front of your mother to protect her.

When the lid pops open, the outside light is blinding. All you can see is a dark shadow standing before you. Strong hands reach in and lift you from the chest, but you do not struggle.

The man sets you down on the beach. "Are you okay?" he asks.

You blink against the sunlight. Slowly your eyes adjust to the brightness. The man before you is tall and strong. His beard is scruffy. His clothes are ragged. His hands are rough and dirty. You can tell by the faint smell of fish that he is a fisherman.

"What a fine young lad," the man says with a smile. "Protecting your mother."

His face is kind, and you feel all worry leak from your body. Now you are simply tired. Very, very tired.

The man turns to your mother, who is still crouched in the chest.

"My name is Dictys," he says as he extends a hand to her. "Welcome to the island of Seriphus."

Dictys helps your mother from the chest and asks her what happened. How did she and her son end up locked in a chest and adrift at sea? Your mother tells the story of King Acrisius, and she introduces you.

"That is a sad tale," he whispers. "I will find you some clean clothes and food to eat back at my hut."

Go to the next page.

Dictys's home is small, and the food he has to offer isn't much, but at least you don't starve.

After several days, you and your mother regain your strength. You begin to help Dictys fish. You even enjoy tossing the nets out into the water and hauling them back in, heavy with fish.

While you're fishing, Dictys asks, "Have you heard the story of Medusa?"

"Yes," you answer. "She has snakes for hair."

"Did you know that she was once very beautiful?"

"No," you reply.

"Medusa fell in love with Poseidon, the powerful god of the sea," says Dictys. "He and Medusa would meet secretly in Athena's temple."

"Isn't Athena the goddess of war?" you ask.

"She's more than that," Dictys explains. "She's the goddess of heroes. She helps them on their quests. She's also wise, which is why one of her symbols is the owl.

"Athena wasn't happy that Medusa was meeting Poseidon in her temple. She couldn't punish Poseidon. So she turned her vengeance on Medusa. Athena changed her from a beautiful woman to a monster.

"Medusa's hair turned into venomous snakes. Her fingernails grew into claws. Her teeth became long, sharp tusks. Now she is so hideous that anyone who looks upon her face turns to stone. They say she lives in a faraway land with her two equally horrible sisters, the Gorgons."

"I sure wouldn't want to make Athena mad," you say. "She doesn't sound like a nice goddess."

"Young Perseus," Dictys says, "as long as you respect the gods, they will not harm you."

One day, as you and your mother are helping Dictys with chores, three men approach. The lead man wears a crown and fine robes. The men behind him appear to be guards. They carry long spears and wear armor.

"My brother, Dictys," the man wearing the crown says. "I've heard that you pulled a chest from the sea. I'm here to see what treasures the gods have given you and to claim my share as king."

Dictys turns to you and your mother. "That is Polydectes, my brother and the ruler of Seriphus." Then facing his brother, Dictys continues. "I didn't find any treasure in the chest. Just these two: Danae and her son, Perseus."

Polydectes slowly studies you and your mother. You grow uncomfortable under his gaze.

"They are treasures in themselves," the king says. "Perseus looks like a strong lad, and his mother is very beautiful. She'd make a fine queen."

Your mother thanks the king for his kind words.

"I hope my brother has treated you well," the king says to your mother.

"Yes, he has," your mother replies.

"I've done my best with what little I have," Dictys says. "They have recovered from their ordeal at sea."

"And I am grateful of that," the king says. "But guests to our island deserve better than a filthy shack to sleep in." Polydectes looks into your mother's eyes. "I invite you and your son to live with me in my palace."

Your mother turns to you. She looks unsure about what to say. "What would you like to do?" she asks.

Dictys has treated you well. He's offered his home and food to you, and you feel as if you owe him your life. But your mother is used to living in a palace, not in a fisherman's hut. While you like Dictys, you're not sure that your mother is happy here. In Polydectes's palace, you both could lead a comfortable life. What will you choose to do?

To stay with Dictys, go to page 49.

To live with Polydectes, go to page 78.

You are thankful that you chose the winged sandals. They are what Hermes uses to fly around as messenger of the gods. Without them, it could take a long time to reach the land where Atlas holds up the heavens. With them, it will be a matter of minutes.

"Just think about where you want to go," Hermes tells you. "The sandals will take you there."

You think of Atlas. The wings on your sandals begin to flutter. First your left leg and then your right lifts off the ground. You wobble as you struggle to keep your balance, but slowly you rise upward.

You're not sure if this is safer than walking, but it's too late. You are a hundred feet off the ground. The only way to go is onward.

You lean in the direction you want to fly. You hear the wings begin to whir, and you are pushed forward with the wind whipping your hair. The ground below you becomes a blur.

3
THE GRAY WITCHES

As you leave Seriphus, the world below you turns a deep blue. You see ships with sails puffed out in the breeze. You see birds soaring overhead and dolphins darting through the waves. You zip by it all unseen.

You cross the Mediterranean Sea faster than a fish can swim, quicker than a ship can sail, and speedier than a bird can fly.

The water turns from deep blue to a lighter blue. The coast of Africa is ahead. The land is green, while miles inland, a large desert spreads across the continent.

You follow the coast eastward, toward a long range of mountains. You head for the highest peak. As you near its heights, you see Atlas towering above the world.

You remember hearing of Atlas and his people, the Titans, through stories Dictys told you. The Titans were a race of powerful giants. They ruled the world before Zeus and the other gods did.

Atlas was the strongest of the Titans and the leader of their army. When Zeus defeated the Titans, he forced Atlas to hold the heavens above the earth forever.

You land next to the giant. His muscles strain. Sweat drips from his brow.

"What do you want, mortal?" he grunts.

"I'm searching for the Gray Witches," you reply. "I've been told that they live in these mountains."

"If I help you find them, will you do me a favor?" the Titan asks.

"What is it?" you ask.

"I've been holding up the heavens for ages," Atlas says. "I need to put some padding on my shoulders and stretch my stiff back. If you could hold the heavens for a moment, I will tell you where the Gray Witches are."

You look around. The mountain range stretches far to the west and east. Finding the Gray Witches could take years, and Polydectes is planning to marry your mother in a month. But Atlas is an enemy of your father, Zeus. You aren't sure if you can trust him. What will you choose to do?

To help Atlas, go to page 46.

To refuse his request, go to page 70.

Now that you are this close to your goal, you want your quest to end as quickly as possible. You fly to the top of the hill.

A puff of dust surrounds your feet as you land. The ground is as dry as stone. Actually, the ground is stone. There's no color to be seen. Just gray.

The area is peppered with tall columns of rock. You hide behind one of them, and you are stunned to notice that the rock column is the shape of a person. Part of the face has been worn away by wind, but you can still see the expression of terror.

Next to that, you notice a large boulder—or at least what you thought was a boulder. It's a stone horse. A stone rider lies on the ground next to it.

You hear voices approaching.

"Where's our sister?" one hisses.

"Moping in her cave," another voice crackles.

They must be talking about Medusa. You can learn where to find her from them. You strap your shield to your arm and draw your sword. You don't know if these women will be friendly, but Medusa is nearby. You'll prepare for the worst.

You step out bravely from your hiding place. "Tell me where to find Medusa," you command.

They stop. That's when you notice that they have snakes for hair, just like Medusa. They also have long, sharp claws instead of fingers.

"Who goes there?" one of them spits.

"I am Perseus," you reply.

"We've heard of you," the other one screeches, "from our sisters, the Gray Witches."

Sisters? These must be Medusa's other sisters, the Gorgons. One of them whirls around, and razor-sharp talons swing toward your face. You raise your shield just in time to deflect the blow.

Clang!

You swing your sword at the Gorgon who attacked. As your blade arcs through the air, the other Gorgon reaches out and catches it in her hands.

Thunk!

It's as if she is made of stone.

"Hee, hee, hee," the Gorgon cackles.

"Don't you know? We Gorgons are immortal," the other Gorgon laughs.

They can't be killed? You look at the hands that clasp your sword. Then you turn your gaze upward to her face. When you do, you are horror struck. She is the most disgusting, the most frightening, the most terrible thing you have ever seen.

Fear overwhelms you, and you cannot move. You just stare back at her yellow eyes.

"Another hero for our statue garden," says a Gorgon.

"We must show it to Medusa," the other cackles.

Even though they're right in front of you, their voices fade to silence. Grayness creeps into the edges of your vision and slowly covers your sight. Your arms and legs are frozen in place. You have been turned to stone by the horrible sight of the Gorgons.

Go to the next page.

THE END

TRY AGAIN

You strap your shield onto one arm and draw the sword that Hermes gave you. Slowly, so as not to make a sound, you approach the witch with the eye. When you get close to her, you jab the sword into her back. She flinches in pain.

"Who's there," she screams as she whirls around.

"My name is Perseus," you answer.

"And what do you want, young man?" she asks.

"I'm on a quest to slay Medusa. I need you to tell me where to find her."

The witch screeches, "Why should I tell you where my sister lives?"

"Because I will use this sword if you don't."

"You're not a very brave one," she says. "Threatening an old woman with Hermes's sword."

"How do you know whose sword this is?" you ask.

"And is that Athena's shield?" she teases.

"Yes," you say.

The witch cackles. And that's when you realize your mistake. You were too focused on the witch with the eye. You thought the others would be helpless because they can't see. You were wrong.

Drawn to the sound of your voice, one witch grabs your shield. She is stronger than you imagined. She rips the shield from your grip.

The witch with the tooth leans forward and bites your hand. You scream in pain, and your sword clatters to the ground at your feet.

The two witches grab you by your arms and legs. They lift you overhead with an iron grip. No matter how hard you wiggle, you cannot escape.

"Sisters, bring him here," the witch with the eye calls. "It will be nice to have some fresh meat in our stew tonight."

The witches carry you to the pot, and they drop you into it with a *splash*. The lid *clangs* down above you. You have just become the witches' dinner.

Go to page 67.

It may take a lot of work to find the Gray Witches, but you decide not to trust Atlas. You worry that an enemy of your father might be an enemy to you as well.

You turn from Atlas. The wings on your sandals whir as you launch into the air. You hover for a moment and scan the horizon. You do not know where to go, but by flying above the mountains, you might spot a clue.

Go to the next page.

The minutes pass, and then the hours. You grow frustrated, but your mother is depending on you. You can't give up.

Just before nightfall, you see an owl circling near a cliff face. It could be looking for mice. Or it could be a sign from Athena.

You swoop toward the owl—and you see a dark cave along the cliff face. You land on a narrow ledge outside the cave. You hear voices coming from inside. You lean closer and listen.

"Mmmm, dinner looks tasty."

"Let me see!"

You peek into the cave.

Three elderly women sit around a large black pot: the Gray Witches. One of them stirs it, and you think you see human bones float to the surface of their stew.

"It's almost ready," the first witch says loudly.

"My turn. Give me the eye," the second demands.

You watch as the first witch reaches two fingers into her eye socket. Then with a loud *slurp*, she pulls out the eye and hands it to the second witch.

With a *pop*, the second witch pushes the eye into an empty eye socket. She blinks several times before the pupil of the eye faces outward. "Yes, it looks about ready," she cackles.

"Who would like a taste?" the first witch asks.

"Me, me, me," the third witch replies.

The second witch opens her mouth. One large tooth hangs from her gums. She grabs the tooth and wiggles it. With a *smuck*, it comes loose. She hands it to the third witch, who takes the tooth and *snaps* it into her gums. She smiles a horrible smile.

The first witch holds up the spoon. The bones of a paw are on it. The witch with the tooth flails blindly for the spoon, grabs it, and pulls it toward herself. She slurps up the broth and sucks up the bones. *Crunch! Crunch! Crunch!* They crack as she chews.

After swallowing, she exclaims, "Delicious!"

"My turn," the first witch says, and they exchange the tooth again.

The rest of the cave looks empty, although the fire under the pot is not very bright. The walls of the cavern are hidden in a curtain of shadow.

You must do something, but you're not sure what. You could sneak up on the witches. You might even overhear them talking about Medusa. Or you could force the witches to tell you. You have weapons, after all. Should you be patient and sneaky? Or should you be bold and brave? What will you choose to do?

To sneak up on the witches, go to page 24.

To threaten the witches, go to page 48.

You turn your back and walk away. You don't want to be bothered, especially by one of the people who laughed at you.

She calls your name again.

"Go away," you snap. "I don't need your help."

A blinding flash of light explodes in front of you. Within the light, that same woman appears. But she's no ordinary woman. You now recognize her as Athena, a goddess.

"How dare you disrespect me!" she yells.

Her voice is deafening. You cover your ears as you fall to your knees.

"I was going to help you on your quest," she says. "But now let's see how you do without my aid."

There's another brilliant flash of light. Instead of standing outside Polydectes's palace, you find yourself in a barren landscape. There are no trees, no flowers, no grass. Everything is gray. Everything is stone.

You begin to recognize shapes in the stone. What you thought was a stone pillar is really a man. What you thought was a huge boulder is a horse—its stone rider lying next to it.

Hissss!

You turn in time to see the most disgusting, the most frightening, the most terrible thing you could ever imagine. Fear overwhelms you. You try to scream, but no sound comes out. You try to raise your hands to cover your eyes, but your arms are heavy and unmoving.

Your eyes cloud over, and you are stuck in place. You have been frozen, and now you are just another statue in Medusa's rock garden.

Go to page 67.

If you steal their tooth, the witches will not be able to eat. More importantly, it seems to be the only real weapon they have.

"Don't eat it all," the third witch says. "Let me taste it again."

With a *smuck*, the second witch pulls the tooth from her gums. She hands it to her sister, who reaches blindly for it.

Before she can find it, you reach in and snag the tooth from her.

"Who are you?" the first witch screeches.

"I am Perseus," you answer boldly.

"What do you want from us?" the second witch asks.

"I'm on a quest to slay Medusa, and I need you to tell me where to find her."

The second witch grins, "Why should I tell you where my sister is?"

"Because I have your tooth. Without it you'll starve."

The witch cackles. And that's when you realize your mistake. You were too focused on the witch with the eye. You thought the other witches would be helpless because they can't see. You were wrong.

Drawn to the sound of your voice, one witch grabs your shield. She is stronger than you had imagined. She rips the shield from your grip.

The other witch grabs your sword arm. She twists your wrist, and you scream in pain. Your sword clatters to the ground at your feet.

The two witches pick you up by your arms and legs. They lift you overhead with an iron grip. No matter how hard you wiggle, you cannot escape.

"Sisters, bring him here," the witch with the eye calls. "It will be nice to have some fresh meat in our stew tonight."

The witches carry you to the pot, and they drop you into it with a *splash*. The lid *clangs* down above you. You have just become the witches' dinner.

Go to page 67.

Your mother is a princess. She deserves to live in a castle. For her sake, you will leave with Polydectes.

Both you and your mother hug Dictys goodbye. He has helped you greatly, but you know that your mother would never be happy living in a fishing hut. She's used to having servants do her chores.

Polydectes leads you and your mother to his palace. Your mother says the palace is much smaller than your grandfather's, but it is still lavish. There are fountains and gardens of colorful flowers. Servants scurry to and fro. Guards stand at attention whenever you pass by. You are in awe, and even your mother is impressed.

Before you enter the palace, Polydectes announces his plans for you and your mother. He says that he will marry your mother.

"I— I—," she stutters, visibly shaken. "I don't know what to say."

"Be thankful for this honor. You will be my wife and queen of Seriphus." Polydectes turns to you. "And you, Perseus, are strong. You will work in my stables."

Tears stream down your mother's face, which tell you that she's not happy. Whether it's because she must marry a man she doesn't love or because you will be separated from her, you never get a chance to ask her. Your mother is led away, disappearing into the palace with Polydectes. You are brought to the stables.

The work is hard. And you aren't even invited to your mother's wedding. You and the other stable hands can only listen to the cheers of celebration from outside the palace.

You almost never see your mother. When you do, her face is sad. There are always guards near her. They block your path any time you step in her direction.

You made a terrible mistake. Because of it, you must spend the rest of your lonely life working for Polydectes and missing your mother.

Go to page 67.

If you steal their eye, the witches will not be able to see you. That is probably the safer choice.

"Let me see if it's done," the third witch says.

The second witch digs two fingers into her eye socket. With a *pop*, the eye squirts into her hand. She holds it out to her sister, who blindly gropes for it. But before she can take it, you jump forward and snag the eye.

"Where is it?" the third witch cries.

"I just gave it to you," the second witch spits.

"Did not!"

"Did too!"

You step away from them, holding the eye between your thumb and forefinger.

"I have it," you say.

All three witches turn in your direction and hiss.

"Who are you?" the second witch hisses.

"I am Perseus," you say boldly.

"What do you want from us?" the third witch asks.

"I'm on a quest to slay Medusa, and I need you to tell me where she lives."

"Why should we tell you where our sister lives?" the third witch asks.

"Because I have your eye," you answer. "And if you don't help me, I'll squish it."

"Stop, sisters!" the third witch cries out.

Suddenly, you notice two dark shadows on either side of you. Their outstretched hands retreat back into their dark cloaks.

You are instantly aware of the danger. While the witches may be blind, they are far from helpless. You were too focused on the third witch. You weren't watching the other two.

"Stay where you are," you warn them. "Or I will squish your eye!"

As you talk, you notice that they tilt their heads toward the sound of your voice. That's how the two witches snuck up on you, by listening to you. Luckily, you did not fall into their grasp.

"Now, tell me where can I find Medusa!" you shout.

The witches hiss in unison.

"Fine, fine," one of them answers.

"We will tell you," another says.

"But you must promise to give us our eye back," the third witch says.

"I promise."

"You will find her lair at the end of the earth . . ." the first witch says.

". . . where the sun never shines . . ." the second witch adds.

". . . and the moon is never seen." The third witch finishes.

Then, all together, they yell, "Now give us the eye!"

You've seen how dangerous the witches are without their eye. Imagine how deadly they will be if one of them can see you. Can you trust them not to attack if you give the eye back to them? Or will you break your promise to ensure your safety? What will you choose to do?

To keep their eye, go to page 53.

To give the eye back, go to page 18.

You selected the ring because it would keep you safe from Medusa's snake-hair. With the ring on, you safely pick up Medusa's head. The snakes don't seem to be alive anymore, but you never know.

"Medusa!" A scream erupts from the cave.

"Sister!" A second scream quickly follows.

They must be Medusa's sisters, the Gorgons. You look to see if you can tie Medusa's head to your belt, and that is when you make your mistake. You glimpse Medusa's face.

You are horror struck. It is the most disgusting, the most frightening, the most terrible thing you have ever seen. Fear overwhelms you, and you cannot move.

"Another hero for our statue garden," one of Medusa's sisters hisses.

Grayness creeps into the edges of your vision and slowly covers your sight. You have been turned to stone by the horrible face of Medusa.

Go to page 67.

They may look helpless, but they are witches. You won't get too close to them. You draw an arrow and pull back the bowstring.

"Witches," you yell, "my arrow is aimed at you."

The witch with the eye turns to you. "Such a strong young man you are," she says. "What's your name?"

"I am Perseus, son of Zeus."

"A son of a god? That's why you smell so tasty. Why do you threaten me and my sisters?"

"I'm seeking Medusa's lair," you say.

"For what purpose?" she replies.

Something about her questions makes you nervous. It's as if she's trying to . . . distract you?

Suddenly, you realize your mistake. You have taken your eyes off her sisters. They are no longer beside the pot. You glance left. Then right. You see only shadows.

"Where are the others?" you demand.

The witch cackles in reply.

Beside you, two dark forms quickly appear. Drawn by the sound of your voice, they grab your arms and yank you backward. The bow falls from your hands.

The witches are stronger than you imagined. They hold you by your arms and legs. They lift you overhead with an iron grip. No matter how hard you wiggle, you cannot escape.

"Sisters, bring him here," the witch with the eye calls. "It will be nice to have some fresh meat in our stew tonight."

The witches carry you to the pot, and they drop you into it with a *splash*. The lid *clangs* down above you. You have just become the witches' dinner.

Go to page 67.

Hermes gave you the sword and shield for a reason. Hopefully they will help you against this sea monster.

You struggle to free yourself, but another tentacle swings toward you. You hold out your shield, and the tentacle smacks it.

You swing your shield at the tentacle holding your arm. The shield's edge bites deep into the monster's flesh. The tentacle quivers, flinches, then loosens its grip. You jerk your arm free. Then you slash down at the tentacle wrapped around your ankle.

Your winged sandals push you upward, and you break free from the giant beast. But more tentacles wave dangerously about. There are far more than you could ever defend against. And since defense is not an option, you must attack.

Below you, part of the sea monster's large head pokes above the water's surface. Your winged sandals whir as you lean down. Tentacles swing at you from all directions. They thud off your shield, but you don't stop. You see an opening, where there are no tentacles in your path. You hold out your sword and dive.

Thwunk!

Your sword sinks deep into the monster's skull. You feel the monster shiver and squirm. Then all of its many tentacles splash into the water, and the monster is still.

You pull your sword from its skull and leap into the sky as the monster begins to sink. You watch it slowly disappear below the waves, leaving a trail of bubbles.

Exhausted, you fly to King Cepheus and Queen Cassiopeia. Tears of joy stream from their eyes, as they give you the key to unlock Andromeda's chains.

As quickly as your tired body can move, you return to Andromeda and release her. Your winged sandals hum loudly as you carry her back to shore.

"You saved our daughter," the queen cries.

"Anything in our castle, it's yours," the king adds. "Name your reward."

"All I want is to return home," you answer.

"You must be tired and hungry," Andromeda says.

And you are. So you let them convince you to stay for one night. You will bathe, eat, and get a good night's sleep before returning to your mother.

6
HOME
AGAIN

You awaken feeling rested. Your belly is full, and you've taken a bath. Andromeda even finds you some new clothes, so you won't have to greet your mother in the torn rags you were wearing.

You say your goodbyes to the king and queen, and you thank them for their kindness. Then Andromeda leads you to the beach where you first saw her. She thanks you with a hug and gives you a bag of gold coins.

"This is so you don't have to live a poor fisherman's life when you get home."

You return her thanks. Then it's time for you to leave. Your winged sandals begin to flutter, and you are lifted off the sand. You lean forward, and away you go.

The light-blue water below turns dark as the sea deepens. Ships sail through the waves, birds fly among the clouds, and schools of fish swim below. You zip by it all as you cross the Mediterranean Sea.

As the color of the sea lightens, you begin to see the dots of islands below. You look for the familiar coast of Seriphus and zoom toward it. Your quest is nearly over. There is only one thing left to do: get your mother.

But should you stop and see Dictys first or go straight to Polydectes's palace? Dictys may have important news for you. But why wait when you can go directly to Polydectes? The longer your mother is with the king, the more you worry. What will you choose to do?

To see Dictys first, go to page 140.

To fly straight to the palace, go to page 102.

This is a strange land, so it's better to be prepared than to hurry. You glide down to the foot of the hill.

Nothing lives here. There is no sign of water and no color at all. Just gray. The hill you're about to climb is completely made of rock. It's as if everything were turned to stone.

This must be the realm of Medusa, and that means your quest is near its end, and you are about to face a terrible monster.

If you have the witches' eye, go to page 137.

If you do not have it, go to page 125.

You unsling the bow and arrows from your back and let them fall to the ground. You will trust the spear as your weapon of choice.

Pegasus flies toward the Chimera. The monster spots you when you are about a hundred feet away. It opens its lion's mouth and roars loudly. Then it whips its dragon head around, spraying fire in your direction.

Pegasus dives sideways to avoid the flames and then charges toward the beast. You jab your spear at it. Your attack is blocked by slashing lion claws as Pegasus zooms past the monster.

Pegasus quickly spins around. You charge again, and again you are met with dragon fire. Pegasus easily avoids the flames. You lean in with the spear and are blocked by another flurry of claws.

The battle continues. Each time you and Pegasus dive, you avoid the Chimera's flames. And each time you fly by, you jab at the monster. Sometimes you strike it, but more often, your attacks are deflected by the lion claws.

The blows that you strike don't seem to harm the Chimera. So you try a different approach. You have Pegasus fly close circles around the Chimera, and you strike at the beast whenever you see an opening. Your attacks confuse the monster, and you score several blows.

The beast roars. Then it leaps in your direction. Its claws rake Pegasus's side. The horse snorts in pain and flies out of reach of the Chimera.

Did you choose the wrong weapon? It's too dangerous to get close enough to attack the Chimera with a spear. With the bow, you would be able to shoot arrows from a safe distance. That gives you an idea! You don't have to hold the spear. You can throw it.

You convince Pegasus to fly in closer and circle the Chimera again. With one hand, you hold onto the reins. Your other hand is raised, holding the spear, ready to fling it if you see an opening.

The Chimera spins with you, always keeping the lion head facing you. The dragon head hovers high in the air, always facing you, too.

The lion head roars, and you fling the spear with all your might. As the spear sails through the air, the dragon head shoots fire at it. The wooden shaft of the spear bursts into flames, but the metal spearhead keeps flying forward. It strikes the lion head.

The Chimera staggers backward. Its goat head sags. Its dragon head flops to the ground. Its knees buckle. The Chimera falls to the ground, defeated.

Pegasus lands beside the fallen monster, and the villagers come out from hiding. They are afraid, and many have suffered burns. But there is a light of hope in their eyes. They surround you and thank you.

You return to King Iobates and tell him the good news. As a reward, you ask for all of the gold that you and Pegasus can carry. The king agrees.

You use this treasure to help the people rebuild their homes and villages. Your name will be remembered in stories and myths for ages to come.

Go to page 149.

You reach out and take the net from Athena.

Suddenly, you jolt awake. You don't know how long you've been sleeping, but the temple is now dark inside. A net is curled at your feet. You pick it up, and you remember what Athena told you about Pegasus: Every night the winged horse drinks from the fountain behind the temple.

You hurry outside. Then quietly, you sneak around to the back of the temple. You hear the trickle of water, the stamp of hooves, and a snort. Pegasus is here.

You peek around the corner. Pegasus's back is to you as it dips its head to drink. Its wings are tucked against its sides.

Careful not to make a sound, you step out from behind the temple. You whirl the net above your head as you wait for just the right moment.

Pegasus lifts its head, and you let the net fly. The horse rears up, kicking its hooves. It tries to spread its wings, but they get tangled in the net.

Go to the next page.

Suddenly, in a flash of light, Athena appears next to Pegasus. "Shhh," she says as she strokes the horse's muzzle with one hand. "Bellerophon is brave. He will take care of you."

In her other hand, she holds a golden bridle. "Pull the net off," she says to you.

You do as she asks, and then she straps the bridle around the horse's head. She hands the bridle's reins to you and says, "You have earned the right to ride Pegasus. He will serve you loyally against the Chimera."

"How am I to find the Chimera?" you ask.

"Silly mortal," she replies, "look."

Off in the distance, the horizon glows red with fires started by the Chimera. All you'll need to do is follow the path of destruction.

You turn to thank Athena, but she is gone.

Holding the reins, you leap onto Pegasus's back. "It's time to find the Chimera," you say.

The horse seems to understand. It spreads its wings wide. With one mighty flap, you are airborne. You rise higher and higher with each beat of Pegasus's wings. Soon you are hundreds of feet above the ground.

Scanning the landscape, you see a bright flame flare up. That's where the Chimera must be.

You lean in that direction, and Pegasus takes your cue. The horse's powerful wings carry you faster than any horse could run. In a matter of moments, you reach a burning farm.

Below, you see the Chimera. It is more horrible than you ever imagined. Not only does it have a lion's head, but a goat's head sticks up from its goat body, and a dragon's head is at the tip of its dragon tail.

Go to the next page.

You must now prepare for battle, and you'll only be able to use one weapon. The spear is a sturdy tool, but you'll have to fly close to the Chimera to use it. With the bow and arrows, you won't have to get close to the fire-breathing Chimera, but will the wooden arrows be able to pierce the monster's hide? What will you choose to do?

To use the spear, go to page 91.

To use the bow and arrows, go to page 128.

Slaying Medusa will be difficult enough. You do not want to risk getting close to her and being turned into stone, so you arm yourself with your bow.

You pull an arrow from the quiver strapped to your back. Tugging at the bowstring, you are ready.

"Where are you, my young hero?" says Medusa. Her voice sounds closer.

Her feet shuffle against the rocky ground. Her claws scrape the stone people.

Your heart thumps loudly in your chest. Sweat slicks the palms of your hands as you hold the bow steady. You must do something quickly, or she'll find you. But you can't just stand in the open to aim your arrow. If you do, Medusa will see you.

At your feet, you notice a few small rocks. You pick one up and throw it at a statue about twenty feet away. It *tinks* off the stone.

"There you are," Medusa whispers.

She rushes to the statue. Her back is to you, so you step out from your hiding place. You aim and are about to let the arrow fly.

One of the vipers in Medusa's hair hisses at you. Medusa turns. She is the most disgusting, the most frightening, the most terrible thing you've ever seen.

Fear overwhelms you. You try to scream, but no sound comes out. You try to raise your hands to cover your eyes, but your arms are heavy and unmoving.

Your eyes cloud over, and you are stuck in place. You have been frozen, and now you are just another statue in Medusa's rock garden.

Go to page 67.

Whatever is happening below, it is not your concern. You've completed your quest. The only thing that matters now is getting home to stop Polydectes from marrying your mother.

You fly as fast as you can. Within minutes, you see the Mediterranean Sea's blue waters beneath you. The water gets darker as you fly farther out to sea. Then, just as quickly, the water grows lighter again. Soon, you spot land ahead.

As you near the shore, a giant water spout shoots up from the water's surface and grabs you like a huge hand. You struggle against its liquid grip, but you cannot free yourself.

A second water spout shoots into the air, and a giant face forms within it. The only being with the power to do this is Poseidon, god of the sea.

"You are mine, Perseus," Poseidon booms. "You were under Athena's protection—until you chose not to save the woman tied to the rocks. Now you are no longer a hero. So I will punish you for slaying the woman I once loved, Medusa."

Poseidon's face falls back into the sea. Then the water spout that holds you falls, too. But it doesn't let go. It drags you down, down, down.

You crash hard through the surface of the water. You are dazed as you get pulled under. You fight to break free as much as you can, but there is no escape from the clutches of the angry god.

All too soon, water fills your lungs, and your world fades to black forever.

Go to page 67.

It's been weeks since you've seen your mother. You've waited too long, and you're worried about her. You will go straight to Polydectes's palace.

The winged sandals whir as you buzz to the castle. Instead of stopping at the gates, you fly straight over the palace walls. You land in the courtyard.

Looking around, you see that the courtyard is being set up for a feast. Chairs and tables litter the lawn. A band is getting ready at the far end. Servants run from place to place.

"What's going on here?" you ask a passing servant.

"Polydectes is getting married," he replies.

At that moment, Polydectes and your mother step into the courtyard. They are surrounded by six guards.

"Polydectes," you yell. "I have returned!"

Surprise crosses the king's face, but his expression quickly turns to anger. A smile lights up your mother. She cries your name as she runs to you and wraps her arms around you. Tears of joy stream down her face.

The king follows her to you. His guards form a line of spears and armor ahead of him.

"Did you succeed in your quest?" he asks.

"I did," you say, patting the bag tied to your belt.

"No matter. You shouldn't have come back," he sneers. "I will marry your mother, as planned."

The guards point their spears at you.

"Leave this place and swear never to return," orders Polydectes. "Or prepare to die."

"No!" your mother cries.

You have no choice. You must fight. Medusa's head is your best weapon—if it still works. But do you have enough time to remove it from the bag and use it? On the other hand, you've survived this long with just your sword and shield. Are they enough to defeat six trained guards? What will you choose to do?

To use Medusa's head, go to page 118.

To use your sword and shield, go to page 138.

The risk is too great. You're no match for such a monster, and you know it. You decline the king's offer.

"Very well then, leave," the king commands. This time, when the anger darkens his eyes, it is not replaced by a smile.

The guards lead you out of the throne room, back down the hallway, and out of the palace.

As you step into the daylight, you see a woman standing at the gate. You recognize this woman, but she's not really a woman at all. Her owl-shaped broach reveals her true identity. She's Athena, goddess of war and protector of heroes.

"Bellerophon, you disappoint me," she says. "I would have helped you against the Chimera. But since you turned your back on people in need, you will now face the monster alone."

There's a bright flash of white light, and suddenly you're not in Xanthos anymore. You're in the ruins of a village. Burning buildings surround you.

Roar!

You spin to see the Chimera facing you. The creature is more horrible than you ever imagined. Not only does it have a lion's head, but a goat's head sticks up from its goat body, and a dragon's head is at the tip of its dragon tail.

Before you have time to react, the dragon head whips toward you. Flames erupt from its gaping mouth, and fire surrounds you. You have nowhere to run.

The Chimera charges. Its lion's mouth, with sharp teeth glinting in the firelight, opens wide and snarls. Its foot-long claws slash at you.

The attack is too much. You are cut deeply in several places. The dragon head whirls around again, spraying fire everywhere. It is the last sight you ever see.

Go to page 67.

Seeing that the monster has many tentacles, you decide to take flight. It will be easier to avoid all of those tentacles if you are airborne. You just hope that you can distract the monster away from Andromeda.

As you soar toward the monster, several tentacles swing into your path. Your sword easily slices through them, and the monster howls in pain.

For better or worse, you now have its full attention. The monster shifts away from Andromeda. A tentacle swipes at your head. You duck. One goes for your legs. You dart upward. Another swings directly at you. You meet it with your sword.

You dart to and fro, hacking and slashing, blocking and twisting. The sky around you is full of tentacles, but your sandals help you avoid most of them. Those that you can't avoid, you block with your shield. Those that you can't block, you slice apart.

Despite its pain, the sea monster doesn't stop. It must know that you cannot keep up with it for long. A tentacle gets past your defenses. It wraps around one of your ankles. You go to slash at it with your sword, but another tentacle grabs your sword arm.

A strange idea occurs to you. Perhaps you can use Medusa's head against it. You'll have to drop your sword and shield to reach the head, but you might be able to turn the sea monster to stone—if the head still works. But if it doesn't work, you would no longer have any weapons to fight with. Is it worth the risk, or will you continue to fight with sword and shield? What will you choose to do?

To use Medusa's head, go to page 142.

To keep fighting with your sword, go to page 86.

Remembering what Athena told you, you sheathe your sword and strap your shield across your back. You cannot kill the Gorgons, so you must flee. The wings on your sandals whir as you take flight.

You want to look back, but you know you can't. So you fly onward, as fast as the sandals will carry you.

"There!" one of the Gorgons shouts.

"We must avenge our sister," the other answers.

You shoot across the dark sky even faster. The wings of your sandals hum so loudly that you're surprised they stay on your feet.

"Grawwww!" a Gorgon shouts.

You're stunned. It sounds as if they are getting closer. They're catching up to you!

You cannot look at them. You cannot kill them. And you aren't fast enough to get away. It would seem that you're running out of options. But you remember the other gift from the nymphs: the magic helmet. They said it would turn you invisible—just once. With the Gorgons close behind, the time to use it is now.

You grab the helmet, which is strapped to your belt. You pull it over your head.

Nothing seems to change, but the Gorgons buzz right by you. They keep flying, screaming at each other as they race off into the distance.

"Where is he?" one screeches.

"How could he escape?" the other screams.

It worked!

Now, you can return home. You will stop Polydectes from marrying your mother.

5
PRINCESS ANDROMEDA

You have a long journey ahead, so you lean forward and let the wings on your sandals propel you. As you fly north, the sky gets brighter. Black clouds give way to a beautiful blue sky.

Below you, the barren landscape turns into lush, green grasslands teeming with antelope and lions. Then the plants thicken into jungles filled with monkeys.

Instead of flying over Atlas's mountains, you cut across the middle of Africa. This is a more direct route, and it will bring you home more quickly.

You fly over the sweltering Sahara Desert, and you notice that drops of blood drip from your bag. As the drops hit the sand, they sizzle. A snake springs forth from the ground. Medusa's blood is creating thousands of snakes as you zoom over the desert.

You reach the land of Ethiopia. This place is ruled by King Cepheus and Queen Cassiopeia. As you look down, you notice a crowd gathered along the beach. Curiosity gets the better of you, so you swoop down for a closer look.

A line of soldiers separates the people from the rocky shore. Just in front of the soldiers, two royal-looking people stand. They must be King Cepheus and Queen Cassiopeia.

The crowd, the soldiers, the king, and the queen all gaze toward a large rock that juts into the water. A young woman is chained to the rock. She tugs and yanks on the chains, but she is trapped.

Go to the next page.

Your quest is almost complete. You only need to get home with Medusa's head, and your mother will be free from Polydectes. But the woman below appears to be in danger. Should you risk your life to save her? Do you have enough time? Or will you return to your mother right away? What will you choose to do?

To fly home, go to page 100.

To help the woman, go to page 130.

You turn to face the cave entrance, your shield in front of you, your sword raised to attack. You have just defeated Medusa. You will now defeat her sisters.

"What have you done to Medusa?" a voice hisses.

Two creatures emerge from the cave. They look just like Medusa, and their yellow eyes meet your gaze. Fear overwhelms you. You try to scream, but no sound comes out. You raise your hands to cover your eyes, but your arms are heavy and unmoving.

"Another hero for our statue garden," one of the sisters hisses.

Her voice is replaced by a more familiar voice inside your head. *You broke your word to the Gray Witches, Perseus,* says Athena. *You are no hero. This is the cost of that mistake.*

Your eyes cloud over, and you are stuck in place, turned to stone by the horrible sight of the Gorgons.

Go to page 67.

You promised to save Andromeda. The best way to do that is to stay where you are. You strap your shield to one arm. Then you draw your sword. You're ready.

The first of the monster's tentacles swings down at you. You quickly leap aside and chop it with your sword. The monster howls in pain.

You do this again. And again. And again. Yet the monster doesn't stop. You duck under another tentacle, slash yet another, and block one with your shield. The monster never seems to run out of tentacles.

You battle for as long as you can, but soon you grow tired. A tentacle smashes against your shield, and your arm goes numb.

You go to dodge a tentacle swinging down toward you. But you lose your footing on the slippery rock. You wrench your ankle and fall down.

You try to roll out of the way, but a dark shadow covers you just before the heavy tentacle pounds you. The blow that ends your life is struck.

Go to page 67.

It is a good thing you selected the bag. With it, you can safely carry Medusa's head. You carefully slide it into the bag and tie the bag to your belt.

"Medusa!" A scream erupts from the cave.

"Sister!" A second scream quickly follows.

They must be Medusa's sisters, the Gorgons.

If you have the witches' eye, go to page 113.

If you do not have it, go to page 108.

You reach out and take the rope from Athena.

Suddenly, you jolt awake. You don't know how long you've been sleeping, but the temple is now dark inside. A rope is curled at your feet. You pick it up, and you remember what Athena told you about Pegasus: Every night the winged horse drinks from the fountain behind the temple.

You hurry outside. Then quietly, you sneak around to the back of the temple. You hear the trickle of water, the stamp of hooves, and a snort. Pegasus is here.

You take the rope, and you tie one end into a lasso. Then you peek around the corner. Pegasus's back is to you as it dips its head to drink. Its wings are tucked against its sides.

Careful not to make a sound, you step out from behind the temple. You whirl the lasso above your head as you wait for just the right moment.

Pegasus lifts its head, and you let the lasso fly. The rope loops around the horse's head and pulls tight as Pegasus rears up.

Suddenly, Pegasus spreads its wings wide. With one gigantic swoop, the horse is airborne.

In your shock, you hold onto the rope tightly as Pegasus lifts you off the ground. Within seconds, you are hundreds of feet in the air. It's too late to let go, so all you can do is hang on.

Pegasus keeps flying higher and higher. The air turns cold, and your arms begin to ache. Slowly your hands grow numb, but Pegasus doesn't seem to tire.

After what feels like hours, your hands lose their grip. Slowly, you slip down the length of rope. And then the rope is gone, and you are falling.

Go to page 67.

You can beat six guards, but how many more will come if you do? You could flee, but your winged sandals cannot carry both you and your mother away fast enough to avoid their spears. That leaves you with few options, so you must try something desperate.

"Keep your eyes closed," you say to your mother.

Then you turn to Polydectes. "I brought you Medusa's head." You reach into the bag. You feel the limp bodies of dead snakes, and you grab a handful of them. As you pull Medusa's head from the bag, you look away.

The guards' gasps of horror are all you need to hear to know that your trick worked. They've been turned to stone. You stuff Medusa's head back into the bag and then look around. Seven statues stand before you, all with looks of terror twisting their faces.

"You can open your eyes," you tell your mother.

She opens them to the sight of the petrified guards and Polydectes. "You've saved us," she says.

A bright light flashes in front of you, and a beautiful woman appears.

"Athena!" you exclaim.

The goddess glows as she speaks. "Perseus, you have done well on your quest. But there is one last thing you must do for me."

"Anything," you say.

Athena points to the bag at your belt. "Even in death, Medusa's gaze turns people to stone. It's a weapon too dangerous to be left in mortal hands."

You look at Polydectes and his men, and you understand her meaning. You untie the string that holds the bag to your belt, and you hand it to Athena.

Go to page 147.

MORE GREEK NAMES

Greek mythology has countless stories with many different gods, heroes, and monsters. Perseus's myth is one of the most popular, but Athena helped other heroes, too. One such hero was Bellerophon. Can you survive his story?

Bellerophon (*buh-LAIR-uh-fawn*)—a Greek hero

Chimera (*kye-MEER-uh*)—a fire-breathing monster

Iobates (*eye-OH-buh-teez*)—ruler of Xanthos

Pegasus (*PEG-uh-suss*)—a winged horse

Xanthos (*ZAN-thoes*)—King Iobates's city

ATTACK OF
THE CHIMERA

Your name is Bellerophon. You are a Greek warrior looking for adventure. As you near the city of Xanthos, you see burning houses and charred farmland. People huddle along the road in front of their ruined homes. Their clothes are torn, and they look tired and afraid.

You stop to speak with them. "Was there a fire?"

"Worse," a man replies. Blisters and burns cover his hands and arms. "It was the Chimera."

You've heard of this monster. It has the head of a lion, the body of a goat, and the tail of a dragon. It's a fearsome beast that breathes fire.

"The Chimera has been terrorizing all of the nearby villages," a woman adds.

"And our king does nothing," another woman says.

This isn't your land, and these are not your people. But you feel sorry for the families now left hungry and homeless. "I will go and see your king," you promise. "I will ask for his help."

The people respond with cheers.

On your way to the king's palace in Xanthos, you see more charred homes, more destroyed villages, and more homeless people. Yet there aren't any soldiers to be found. No one protects the people from the Chimera.

You reach the edge of the capital city. Its tall walls greet you. Along the top of the walls, soldiers armed with bows and arrows march to and fro.

You enter the city through its main gate. Ahead of you, the palace stands, surrounded by more walls and more soldiers. You approach two soldiers guarding the palace gate.

"I wish to speak with the king," you say.

"Why would King Iobates want to speak with you?" one of the guards asks.

The other points a spear in your direction.

"I'm here to talk about the Chimera," you say.

The guards study you for a long moment. You're not sure if they're judging you as a threat or as a fool, but they eventually let you into the palace.

Inside, you are met by two more guards. They lead you down a long hallway and into the throne room. There, you are introduced to the king.

"My name is Bellerophon, a warrior from Greece."

"Welcome to my kingdom," the king replies. "You look like a brave hero."

"I wish to speak about the Chimera," you say.

"Yes, a horrible creature," replies the king. "It's a shame what's happening beyond my palace walls."

"Your people need your help," you say boldly. "You must do something."

A look of anger darkens the king's eyes—but only for a second, before a smile spreads across his face. "Isn't that why you're here, young Bellerophon?" he says. "To be a hero? To battle the Chimera?"

The kings walks over to you and places a hand on your shoulder. "I've been searching for a brave warrior like you," he says. "You can help my people. And if you slay the beast, you will receive any reward you desire. I offer you gold, diamonds, gems, anything—if you kill the Chimera."

This is not what you were expecting. You had hoped the king would gather an army to battle the Chimera, not ask you to kill the monster for him. Unfortunately, it looks as if he cares more about his castle than he does his people.

You've done what you promised to do. You've asked the king for help. You could leave now without feeling guilty. But there are still people who need help. What will you choose to do?

To accept the king's offer, go to page 134.

To refuse the king's offer, go to page 104.

You carefully walk toward the path that leads up the hill. Suddenly, Athena appears before you.

"You have done well so far," she says. "You've acted like a true hero at every turn in your quest. The dangers ahead are the greatest you've faced. Even after you slay Medusa, you will not be safe. She has two sisters, the Gorgons. They are every bit as horrible as she is."

"How so?" you ask.

"Do not look upon them, or you will be turned to stone. And do not fight them. Unlike Medusa, they are immortal. They cannot be killed."

With that warning, Athena disappears.

Go to the next page.

You stalk along the path and up the hill. Rock crunches under your sandals. You could easily fly to the top, but you fear being seen.

As you reach the peak, you are amazed by what you see. Odd-shaped stone columns cover the hilltop. They are scattered everywhere.

You duck behind one, and you notice it is not just a column. This—and all of the others—are statues of people. Many have raised arms. Some look back as if they are running from danger. But the one thing they all have in common is a look of great fear. These are the people who have been petrified by Medusa.

Your knees tremble, and sweat beads on your brow. You want to flee, and it would be easy to do so. You could just fly away. But your mother is waiting for you, and you cannot save her if you do not slay Medusa.

Bravely, you step out from behind the statue and scan the area. In the distance, you see that the path leads to a cave. That must be Medusa's lair.

You hurry toward the cave entrance, and you hear a voice. "Who's there?" a woman calls.

You dart behind another statue.

Screech! It's the sound of claws raking across rock.

"I thought I saw a brave hero coming to fight me," the woman says.

This is the moment you've been waiting for. You've found Medusa, and now it's time to finish your quest. But before you do, you must arm yourself.

If you have the bow and arrows, go to page 98.

If you do not, go to page 144.

You can't risk getting close to the Chimera, so you choose the bow and arrows. You let the spear fall to the ground, and you prepare your bow for battle.

Pegasus flies toward the Chimera. The monster spots you when you are about a hundred feet away. It opens its lion's mouth and roars loudly.

You decide that this is close enough. You take aim and release the arrow. It sails through the air toward its target. But before the arrow gets close, the Chimera's dragon head whips around and sprays fire at it. The arrow turns to ash and falls harmlessly to the ground.

You fire another arrow and another. Each time, the Chimera burns them to dust. You have Pegasus fly a little closer, hoping the Chimera won't be quick enough to fry your next arrow. But the monster is done burning arrows. It turns its attention to you.

It whips its dragon head around, and a thin stream of fire shoots from its mouth. One of Pegasus's wings is set afire. The horse's white feathers quickly burn.

Pegasus lurches to one side, and you are tossed into the air. You only fall about thirty feet, but it is enough. You hurt one of your legs and are unable to walk.

The Chimera pounces. Its lion's mouth, with sharp teeth glinting in the firelight, opens wide and snarls. Its foot-long claws slash at you.

The attack is too much. You are cut deeply in several places. The dragon head whirls around again, spraying fire everywhere. It is the last sight you ever see.

Go to page 67.

You're a hero, and heroes do the right thing. The girl below needs help, so you will provide it.

You fly down to the king and queen. They are quite surprised to see you.

"Why is that girl chained to the rocks?" you ask. "And why won't you help her?"

The king begins to weep and seems unable to speak. So the queen must tell their sad story.

"I am Queen Cassiopeia. I angered Poseidon, the god of the sea, when I bragged that my daughter was more beautiful than his sea nymphs. To punish me, Poseidon has sent a sea monster to destroy our kingdom."

You shake your head. "What does this have to do with that girl?"

The queen continues. Her voice sounds empty and defeated. "She is our daughter, Princess Andromeda. Poseidon said that the only way to save our kingdom is to sacrifice her to the sea monster. She is chained to the rock so that the sea monster will take her away and spare our kingdom."

You don't understand how these people can do this to their own daughter. But you won't let it happen.

"I am going to save Andromeda," you tell the king and queen.

A glimmer of hope shines in the king's eyes, but the queen becomes stern. "You cannot," she demands. "The sea monster will destroy my kingdom."

You don't care what the queen says. You leap into the air and fly to the rock where Andromeda is chained. You land next to her.

"Who are you?" she asks. "Why are you here?"

"My name is Perseus, and I'm going to save you." You tug on the chains wrapped around Andromeda's wrists, waist, and ankles.

"But the sea monster . . ." Her voice is a mix of fear and relief.

You focus on the old, rusty chains that hold her to the rock. As you yank and tug at them, Andromeda squirms in pain. She's bound tightly.

You can't hack at the chains with your sword—you might harm her. But you can't break the chains with your hands either.

You turn your attention to a large lock near her feet. If only you had asked for the key. But you're not sure

Cassiopeia would have given it to you. She seems set on sacrificing her daughter.

"Please, hurry," Andromeda pleads.

You hammer at the lock with the bottom of your sword as loud *chings* echo across the bay. The lock holds. Your efforts barely dent the rusted metal.

"Oh, no," Andromeda gasps. "It's too late!"

Go to the next page.

You turn to face the sea. Its waters explode in every direction as monstrous tentacles shoot skyward. There are so many, and they are so huge, that they block out the sun.

There's no longer any time to free Andromeda. You must now face Poseidon's sea monster. Should you stay where you are to better protect Andromeda? Or should you fly upward and move into a better attack position? What will you choose to do?

To stay where you are, go to page 114.

To fly up and attack, go to page 106.

You are a hero. It is your duty to help people in need. If the king won't do anything for them, then this task must fall to you.

"I have weapons for you," the king offers.

The two guards approach. One holds a bow and a quiver of arrows. The other presents a spear.

"Take them. They will help you slay the Chimera," the king says.

"I accept your offer," you reply. You sling the quiver of arrows across your back, along with the bow. You take the spear in hand.

You nod and say, "Thank you." Then you follow the guards out of the palace.

As you step into the daylight, an old man walks by. His robes are torn and tattered, but you notice an owl tattooed to the man's arm.

"I'm here to help you," he whispers.

You recognize the owl as one of Athena's symbols. She is the protector of heroes, and you're hoping that she'll help you on your quest. So you listen to what the man has to say.

"Go to Athena's temple, outside the city's walls. There, you will receive items to help on your quest."

You do as the old man says. You exit the city and go straight to Athena's temple. You are surprised to find it completely empty, so you sit down and wait. And wait. And wait.

Hours later, your head grows heavy. Your eyes close. You fall asleep and dream.

In your dream, Athena approaches you. She is surrounded by shimmering light, and she floats above you. She holds two objects: a rope and a net.

"Brave Bellerophon, I'm here to aid you on your quest," she says. "To slay the Chimera, you will need a steed as brave as you. You will need to ride Pegasus."

You've heard stories of this winged horse. The stories say it was born from the blood of Medusa after Perseus cut off her head.

"Only by riding Pegasus will you be able to battle the Chimera," says Athena. "Pegasus will keep you out of reach of Chimera's fiery breath."

"Will Pegasus help me?" you ask.

"If you can catch Pegasus, it will help you," she replies. "Every night, Pegasus comes to drink from the fountain behind my temple. I offer you a choice: a rope or a net to capture Pegasus. Choose wisely."

If you choose the rope, go to page 116.

If you choose the net, go to page 94.

You reach into your pocket and pull out the eye you stole from the witches. You remember their curse, and you feel a flicker of worry.

You gaze into the eye. Its black pupil contracts as it stares back at you. Can the witches see you through it? You stuff the eye back into your pocket. It's best not to think about it.

Go to page 126.

You pull your mother behind you to protect her. Then quickly, you unsling your shield from your back and draw your sword. It's six against one, but you're not afraid. After all, you've already defeated Medusa and a sea monster.

A guard thrusts his spear at you. With one hack of your sword, you chop off its tip. Two more guards attack. You block one's spear with your shield. The other, you swipe at with your sword.

The remaining three guards charge. One jabs at your feet. You leap over his spear. Another thrusts at your head. You duck. The third aims his spear at your belly, and you block it with your shield.

The fighting is fierce and fast. You stab and block as the guards jab and thrust. You block one spear, and then another stabs at your chest. You attack one of the guards, and two more defend him.

Slowly, the battle turns in your favor. Only two uninjured guards remain. You can win this!

Your hopeful thoughts are quickly dashed. Dozens more guards stream out of the palace, drawn to the sounds of combat.

You could flee, but your winged sandals cannot carry both you and your mother away fast enough to avoid those spears. You have no choice but to fight.

You last for as long as you can, but there are too many of them.

A spear tip sinks deep into your chest. Your knees give out, and you collapse to the ground. The last thing you see is your mother hovering over you. Her face is streaked with tears.

Go to page 67.

Dictys has been your one true friend. You need to see him before you do anything else.

You find him along the beach. He drops his fishing net as he sees you, and he greets you with a hug.

"Perseus, you're back," he shouts. "Did you . . ." His voice trails off.

"I did," you say, patting the bag tied to your belt.

A look of astonishment crosses his face. "I wasn't sure I'd ever see you again," Dictys says with a hint of sadness in his voice.

"I couldn't fail," you reply. "Athena helped me."

As Dictys leads you toward his hut, he asks about your adventures. But you have more important things on your mind. You want to know how your mother is.

"Polydectes plans to marry your mother tonight," he says, his eyes cast downward. "He's told everyone, even your mother, that you are surely dead—that no one can survive Medusa."

Anger boils within you. You want to storm to the palace and demand that Polydectes return your mother.

"The king has many guards," Dictys says. "You can't just walk in. They will kill you."

You shake your head. "I could sneak into the palace by flying over the walls."

You reach Dictys's hut, but suddenly a dozen soldiers rush out of it. They point their spears at you.

"What are you doing here?" Dictys asks.

The soldiers ignore him. Instead, their leader turns to you. "The king knew you'd come back here first. He wants us to make sure you fail in your quest."

You barely have time to draw your sword before the guards attack. The fighting is fierce and fast. You block and hack as the soldiers jab with their spears. You last for as long as you can, but there are too many of them.

A spear tip sinks deep into your chest. Your knees give out, and you collapse to the ground. The last thing you see is Dictys hovering over you. His face is streaked with tears.

Go to page 67.

You are desperate and in trouble. At this point, anything is worth a try.

You drop your sword and cast your shield aside. With your free hand, you dig into the bag. You feel the limp bodies of the snakes, and you grab a handful of them.

The sea monster's tentacles pull you down toward its toothy mouth. As they do, another tentacle wraps around your chest. It constricts, and the breath is squeezed from your lungs. You must act swiftly.

You close your eyes as you pull Medusa's head from the bag. You hold the head in front of you, toward the sea monster.

At first, nothing happens. Then you feel the tentacles stiffen, and you stop moving downward.

You quickly tuck Medusa's head back into the bag before daring to open your eyes. You see the tentacles slowly turn to the dead gray of stone.

Tentacles are still wrapped around your arm, your ankle, and your chest. They turn to stone around you, and you are stuck within their grasp.

Slowly at first, you feel the tentacles start to sway. Then faster and faster. The sea monster begins to tip.

You crash hard through the surface of the water. You are dazed as you get pulled under. You fight to break free for as long as you can, but there is no escape from the stone grasp of the sea monster.

All too soon, water fills your lungs, and your world fades to black forever.

Go to page 67.

There must be a reason Hermes gave you his sword and Athena's shield. You arm yourself with them.

"Where are you, my young hero?" taunts Medusa. Her voice sounds closer.

You hear the crunch of gravel under her feet and the hiss of her snake-hair. There is a *whoosh*, as razor-sharp claws slice through the air.

Your instincts tell you to duck, so you do. A loud screech fills your ears as Medusa's claws rake across the rocky statue just above your head.

Without looking back, you run and hide behind the nearest statue.

"You can't hide forever," Medusa calls.

You hear her footsteps coming toward you again, so you dash to the next statue. Seconds later, you hear the hiss and the scrape of talons cutting the statue you were just behind.

Medusa is right. You can't hide forever. But you can't fight her either—not when you can't even look at her.

Whoosh!

You raise your shield just as Medusa's claws arc down toward your throat. There's a clang as you deflect the blow. That's when you notice your reflection staring back at you. The inside of your shield is polished. It acts as a mirror.

You race away from Medusa, and you dive behind another statue.

"Don't run from me," Medusa jeers. "I just want to look at you, my brave hero." She laughs wickedly.

You can't keep running around like this. Eventually, you will accidentally look at her, and that will be the end of you. You need a plan.

You glance at the back of the shield and see your blurry reflection. It gives you an idea. Instead of peeking out to see where Medusa is, you can use the shield, like a mirror, to peek around the statue. Then you won't risk looking at her and being turned to stone.

You listen as Medusa's footsteps draw closer. It's time to attack.

"I know where you're hiding," Medusa says.

You hold your shield in front of you and study the mirror's image. First you see a hand with razor claws, then a scaly arm, a shoulder, and above that, a swarm of vipers. Their tongues flick the air.

You judge that Medusa is five feet from you now. You grip your sword and inhale deeply. Then you close your eyes, leap from your hiding spot, and swing at where you think Medusa's neck is.

You feel your blade make contact. There's a hiss! Then a scream, "Ahhhh!" That's followed by the thud of something hitting the ground.

You open your eyes. The headless body of Medusa lies at your feet. A few feet from there, her head faces away from you. The vipers have stopped their wiggling.

If you have the nymphs' ring, go to page 83.

If you have the nymphs' bag, go to page 115.

EPILOGUE: THE RIGHT CHOICE

You're back in the library. You aren't sure what just happened. Dictys, the Gray Witches, Medusa, the sea monster, was it all a dream?

Dream or not, a part of you has changed. You dig the wallet out of your pocket. Then you go in search of the boy who dropped it.

You find him at the front desk, asking if anyone has found his missing wallet. You step over to him and hold it out in front of him.

"You dropped this," you say.

He looks up, sees what's in your hand, and smiles. "Thanks, man," he says as he takes it from you.

You're about to turn away and go back to your book when he asks, "You like *Muscle Man*?"

"Yeah," you reply.

"He's one of my favorites," the older boy says.

"What are you reading?" you ask.

"I got the new *Hercules* graphic novel," he replies. "You should check it out. I snagged the newest issue, but the first couple are over on the shelf."

"Thanks, maybe I will," you say.

The older boy thanks you again, says goodbye, and walks off.

You return to your chair to read your book. You feel good about yourself and what you just did. It's what a hero would have done.

You think about Perseus. He wasn't a hero because of super powers or magic weapons. He was a hero because he always chose to do the right thing. You aren't much different than he was. You have the power to do the right thing, too.

Go to the next page.
(Or for another adventure, go to page 120!)

The End

You survived Greek Mythology's Adventures of Perseus

Did you die? How many times?
Tell us at **www.Lake7Creative.com**
(Look for the "I Survived" button.)

WHAT HAPPENS NEXT

When King Acrisius found out about Perseus, he was afraid because of what the gods had told him. But he couldn't kill his grandson because it would anger the gods. That's why he had Danae and Perseus locked in a chest and thrown into the ocean. He hoped to never see them again.

After his quest, Perseus went in search of his grandfather. He wanted to forgive him for what he'd done. But when King Acrisius heard that Perseus was looking for him, he was afraid and fled his kingdom.

Perseus and Acrisius both ended up in the city of Larissa. The city was holding special games. When the people saw that Perseus was a strong young man, they asked him to join the games.

Perseus took part in the discus competition. But when he threw the discus, it slipped from his hand and sailed into a crowd. Acrisius was in that crowd. The discus struck and killed him. The gods' prediction had come true, but it turned out to be an accident.

ABOUT MYTHS

In ancient times, storytellers would go from village to village telling stories. These stories, or myths as we now call them, would be passed from person to person and would be retold over and over again.

During the retellings, storytellers often changed things. They would make the monsters more horrifying, the heroes braver, the fights more dramatic. They did this to keep their audiences entertained. The more excited people were to hear the stories, the more popular the storytellers would be.

That is why there are so many different versions of some myths. Throughout the years, storytellers created their own versions of the most popular myths. For example, in some retellings of Perseus's story, he rides a winged horse named Pegasus. In others, he uses winged sandals to fly from place to place. Even in this book, some of the story's details have been changed.

All of these unique versions are what continue to make ancient myths so interesting. Each storyteller has his or her own interpretation of the story.

ABOUT THE AUTHOR

Blake Hoena grew up in central Wisconsin. In his youth, he wrote stories about robots conquering the moon and trolls lumbering around in the woods behind his parents' house. The fact that the trolls were hunting for little boys had nothing to do with Blake's pesky brothers. Later, he moved to Minnesota to pursue a Master of Fine Arts degree in Creative Writing from Minnesota State University, Mankato.

Since graduating, Blake has written more than fifty books for children. Currently he is working on more Choose Your Path books.